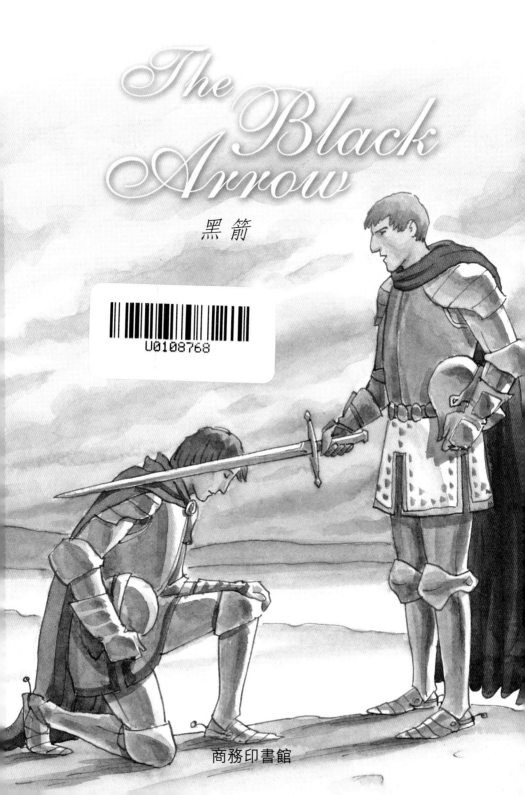

The Black Arrow

黑箭

商務印書館

This Chinese edition of *The Black Arrow*
has been published with the written permission of
Black Cat Publishing.

The copyright of this Chinese edition is owned by
The Commercial Press (H.K.) Ltd.

Name of Book: The Black Arrow
Author: Robert Louis Stevenson
Retold by: George Gibson
Activities by: Stuart Cochrane
Editors: Victoria Bradshaw, Michela Bruzzo
Design and art direction: Nadia Maestri
Computer graphics: Simona Corniola
Illustrated by: Alfredo Belli
Picture research: Laura Lagomarsino
Edition: ©2006 Black Cat Publishing,
         an imprint of Cideb Editrice, Genoa, Canterbury

系 列 名：Black Cat 優質英語階梯閱讀 · Level 1
書　　名：黑　箭
責任編輯：畢　琦
封面設計：張　毅
出　　版：商務印書館（香港）有限公司
　　　　　香港筲箕灣耀興道 3 號東滙廣場 8 樓
　　　　　http://www.commercialpress.com.hk
發　　行：香港聯合書刊物流有限公司
　　　　　香港新界大埔汀麗路 36 號中華商務印刷大廈 3 字樓
印　　刷：中華商務彩色印刷有限公司
　　　　　香港新界大埔汀麗路 36 號中華商務印刷大廈
版　　次：2007 年 5 月第 1 版第 1 次印刷
　　　　　© 2007 商務印書館（香港）有限公司
　　　　　ISBN 978 962 07 1822 9
　　　　　Printed in Hong Kong

出版說明

　　本館一向倡導優質閱讀，近年來連續推出了以"Q"為標識的"Quality English Learning 優質英語學習"系列，其中《讀名著學英語》叢書，更是香港書展入選好書，讀者反響令人鼓舞。推動社會閱讀風氣，推動英語經典閱讀，藉閱讀拓廣世界視野，提高英語水平，已經成為一種潮流。

　　然良好閱讀習慣的養成非一日之功，大多數初中級程度的讀者，常視直接閱讀厚重的原著為畏途。如何給年輕的讀者提供切實的指引和幫助，如何既提供優質的學習素材，又提供名師的教學方法，是當下社會關注的重要問題。針對這種情況，本館特別延請香港名校名師，根據多年豐富的教學經驗，精選海外適合初中級英語程度讀者的優質經典讀物，有系統地出版了這套叢書，名為《Black Cat 優質英語階梯閱讀》。

　　《Black Cat 優質英語階梯閱讀》體現了香港名校名師堅持經典學習的教學理念，以及多年行之有效的學習方法。既有經過改寫和縮寫的經典名著，又有富創意的現代作品；既有精心設計的聽、説、讀、寫綜合練習，又有豐富的歷史文化知識；既有彩色插圖、繪圖和照片，又有英美專業演員朗讀作品的 CD。適合口味不同的讀者享受閱讀之樂，欣賞經典之美。

　　《Black Cat 優質英語階梯閱讀》由淺入深，逐階提升，好像參與一個尋寶遊戲，入門並不難，但要真正尋得寶藏，需要投入，更需要堅持。只有置身其中的人，才能體味純正英語的魅力，領略得到真寶的快樂。當英語閱讀成為自己生活的一部分，英語水平的提高自然水到渠成。

商務印書館 (香港) 有限公司
編輯部

使用說明

❶ 應該怎樣選書？

按閱讀興趣選書

《Black Cat 優質英語階梯閱讀》精選世界經典作品，也包括富於創意的現代作品；既有膾炙人口的小説、戲劇，又有非小説類的文化知識讀物，品種豐富，內容多樣，適合口味不同的讀者挑選自己感興趣的書，享受閱讀的樂趣。

按英語程度選書

《Black Cat 優質英語階梯閱讀》現設 Level 1 至 Level 6，由淺入深，涵蓋初、中級英語程度。讀物分級採用了國際上通用的劃分標準，主要以詞彙（vocabulary）和結構（structures）劃分。

Level 1 至 Level 3 出現的詞彙較淺顯，相對深的核心詞彙均配上中文解釋，節省讀者查找詞典的時間，以專心理解正文內容。在註釋的幫助下，讀者若能流暢地閱讀正文內容，就不用擔心這本書程度過深。

Level 1 至 Level 3 出現的動詞時態形式和句子結構比較簡單。動詞時態形式以簡單現在式（present simple）、現在進行式（present continuous）、簡單過去式（past simple）為主，句子結構大部分是簡單句（simple sentences）。此外，還包括比較級和最高級（comparative and superlative forms）、可數和不可數名詞（countable and uncountable nouns）以及冠詞（articles）等語法知識點。

Level 4 至 Level 6 出現的動詞時態形式，以現在完成式（present perfect）、現在完成進行式（present perfect continuous）、過去完成進行式（past perfect continuous）為主，句子結構大部分是複合句（compound sentences）、條件從句（1st and 2nd conditional sentences）等。此外，還包括情態動詞（modal verbs）、被動式（passive forms）、動名詞（gerunds）、短

語動詞（phrasal verbs）等語法知識點。

　　根據上述的語法範圍，讀者可按自己實際的英語水平，如詞彙量、語法知識、理解能力、閱讀能力等自主選擇，不再受制於學校年級劃分或學歷高低的約束，完全根據個人需要選擇合適的讀物。

② 怎樣提高閱讀效果？

　　閱讀的方法主要有兩種：一是泛讀，二是精讀。兩者各有功能，適當地結合使用，相輔相成，有事半功倍之效。

　　泛讀，指閱讀大量適合自己程度（可稍淺，但不能過深）、不同內容、風格、體裁的讀物，但求明白內容大意，不用花費太多時間鑽研細節，主要作用是多接觸英語，減輕對它的生疏感，鞏固以前所學過的英語，讓腦子在潛意識中吸收詞彙用法、語法結構等。

　　精讀，指小心認真地閱讀內容精彩、組織有條理、遣詞造句又正確的作品，着重點在於理解“準確”及“深入”，欣賞其精彩獨到之處。精讀時，可充分利用書中精心設計的練習，學習掌握有用的英語詞彙和語法知識。精讀後，可再花十分鐘朗讀其中一小段有趣的文字，邊唸邊細心領會文字的結構和意思。

　　《Black Cat 優質英語階梯閱讀》中的作品均值得精讀，如時間有限，不妨嘗試每兩個星期泛讀一本，輔以每星期挑選書中一章精彩的文字精讀。要學好英語，持之以恆地泛讀和精讀英文是最有效的方法。

③ 本系列的練習與測試有何功能？

　　《Black Cat 優質英語階梯閱讀》特別注重練習的設計，為讀者考慮周到，切合實用需求，學習功能強。每章後均配有訓練聽、説、讀、寫四項技能的練習，分量、難度恰到好處。

聽力練習分兩類，一是重聽故事回答問題，二是聆聽主角對話、書信朗讀、或模擬記者訪問後寫出答案，旨在以生活化的練習形式逐步提高聽力。每本書均配有 CD 提供作品朗讀，朗讀者都是專業演員，英國作品由英國演員錄音，美國作品由美國演員錄音，務求增加聆聽的真實感和感染力。多聆聽英式和美式英語兩種發音，可讓讀者熟悉二者的差異，逐漸培養分辨英美發音的能力，提高聆聽理解的準確度。此外，模仿錄音朗讀故事或模仿主人翁在戲劇中的對白，都是訓練口語能力的好方法。

閱讀理解練習形式多樣化，有縱橫字謎、配對、填空、字句重組等等，注重訓練讀者的理解、推敲和聯想等多種閱讀技能。

寫作練習尤具新意，教讀者使用網式圖示（spidergrams）記錄重點，採用問答、書信、電報、記者採訪等多樣化形式，鼓勵讀者動手寫作。

書後更設有升級測試（Exit Test）及答案，供讀者檢查學習效果。充分利用書中的練習和測試，可全面提升聽、說、讀、寫四項技能。

◆4 本系列還能提供甚麼幫助？

《Black Cat 優質英語階梯閱讀》提倡豐富多元的現代閱讀，巧用書中提供的資訊，有助於提升英語理解力，擴闊視野。

每本書都設有專章介紹相關的歷史文化知識，經典名著更附有作者生平、社會背景等資訊。書內富有表現力的彩色插圖、繪圖和照片，使閱讀充滿趣味，部分加上如何解讀古典名畫的指導，增長見識。有的書還提供一些與主題相關的網址，比如關於不同國家的節慶源流的網址，讓讀者多利用網上資源增進知識。

Contents

The text is recorded in full.　故事錄音

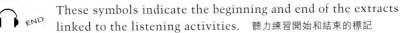

These symbols indicate the beginning and end of the extracts
linked to the listening activities.　聽力練習開始和結束的標記

Robert Louis Stevenson (1892) by Girolamo Pieri Nerli.

About the Author

Robert Louis Stevenson was born in Edinburgh, Scotland, on 13 November 1850. He was not a strong child and was often ill, but he liked the stories about adventures and pirates which his father told him.

In the late 1860s, he went to Edinburgh University. At first he decided to study engineering because his father was an engineer. But Stevenson soon understood that he was not happy with his choice and decided to study law. It was during this time that he became very interested in literature and he began writing stories. Many of these were published in magazines.

In 1876, Stevenson started travelling through Belgium and France, where he met Fanny Osbourne. She was American, eleven years older than himself and a mother of two children. They fell in love immediately, but they did not get married until 1880. After their marriage, they went to live in Scotland with her son, Lloyd.

One day Stevenson started telling Lloyd a story about pirates. This was the beginning of one of Stevenson's most famous stories, *Treasure Island*. This exciting adventure story about pirates and treasure became very popular with children and adults all over the world, and Stevenson became a famous writer. In 1886, he wrote his most famous novel, *The Strange Case of Dr Jekyll and Mr Hyde*. This tells the story of a doctor who drinks a special potion[1] and develops a horrible new personality. His other important novels include: *Kidnapped* (1886), *The Black Arrow* (1888) and *The Master of Ballantrae* (1889).

In 1888, Stevenson was still ill and he felt that the cold, wet, Scottish weather was not good for him. So the family decided to travel to the South Pacific. They spent two years travelling and visited the islands of Hawaii, Tahiti, Samoa and many others. The warm weather helped Stevenson a lot, so the family decided to live in Samoa. Stevenson liked Samoa and the people very much, and they liked him, too. He studied the life and customs of these people and started writing numerous[2] stories set on the islands. Some of these stories were published in a collection called *Island Nights' Entertainments* (1893).

Stevenson died in December 1894 in his home in Samoa. He was only 44 years old. The people of Samoa buried[3] him on top of Mount Vaea.

1 COMPREHENSION CHECK
Are these sentences true (T) or false (F)? Correct the false ones.

		T	F
1	Stevenson liked reading stories as a child.	☐	☐
2	He became an engineer.	☐	☐
3	His wife was French.	☐	☐
4	*Treasure Island* made Stevenson famous.	☐	☐
5	He left Scotland because he was not well.	☐	☐
6	His health did not improve in a warmer country.	☐	☐

1. **potion** : 奇效飲劑。
2. **numerous** : 許多的。

3. **buried** : 埋葬。

9

The Characters

Bennet Hatch

Sir Daniel

Sir Oliver

Ellis Duckworth

John M.

Richard Shelton

Joanna Sedley

Glossary

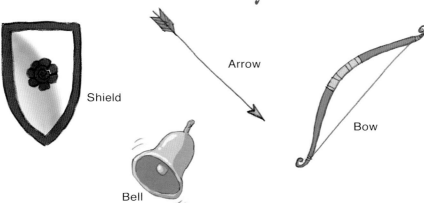

Shield

Arrow

Bow

Bell

Battle

Castle

Forest

Sword

BEFORE YOU READ

1 VOCABULARY

Do you know these words? Write the words from the box under the correct pictures. Use a dictionary to help you.

| priest | village | message |

1 ....

2 ....

3 ....

2 Now complete these sentences with the correct words from the box.

| taxes | defend | loyal |

1 Many years ago, people paid .... to the King. Now we pay them to the government.
2 The soldiers' main job was to .... the castle from attackers.
3 If you are .... to someone, you always help and support them when they need you.

3 LISTENING

Listen to the beginning of the story and answer these questions.

1 When does this story happen?
  A ☐ In the future.
  B ☐ Hundreds of years ago.
  C ☐ In modern times.

2 What's true about England in this story?
  A ☐ People live in peace.
  B ☐ There are no jobs.
  C ☐ There is a war.

3 What's true about the villagers?
  A ☐ They are angry.
  B ☐ They are happy.
  C ☐ They are confused.

Now say why you chose A, B or C for each question.

CHAPTER ONE

The Letter

T he bell of Moat House Castle at Tunstall rang loudly 🎧 one spring afternoon. The people of the village looked up at the castle.

'What's happening?' asked one man.

'I don't know,' said another. 'A messenger brought a letter for Sir Oliver Oates, the priest, half an hour ago. It was from Sir Daniel Brackley.'

'But why is the bell ringing?' asked an old man.

Suddenly a handsome [1] young man appeared on his grey horse. He was about eighteen years old and had brown hair and blue eyes. He had a bow and arrow on his back. His name was Richard Shelton and he was Sir Daniel's ward. [2]

Richard Shelton looked at the people around him and said, 'There will be a big battle soon! Sir Daniel wants everyone to fight.'

'Another battle!' cried an angry woman. 'This is terrible! Our men go and die in battles, and their wives and children are hungry.'

'We pay high taxes to Sir Daniel and we don't have any money for food,' said a young mother with three small children.

'Who is Sir Daniel fighting for today?' asked a tall man. 'Lancaster or York?'

END

'I'm sorry, I don't know,' said Richard, and his face became red.

1. **handsome**：英俊的（用於男性）。
2. **ward**：父母雙亡而受到一名成人監護的兒童。

The Black Arrow

Sir Daniel Brackley was not a loyal man and the people did not like him. He seemed to always change his mind: [1] sometimes he fought for Lancaster and sometimes he fought for York.

A big man on a black horse appeared. It was Bennet Hatch, Sir Daniel's best friend. He was about forty and had dark hair and an unfriendly face.

'All of the men in the village must go to Moat House Castle and get ready for the battle!' Hatch cried.

Then Hatch looked at Richard and said, 'Let's go to Nick Appleyard's house.'

When they arrived Hatch said, 'Nick Appleyard, you must go and defend Moat House Castle because Sir Daniel is going to Kettley to fight.'

While the two men were talking, a black arrow suddenly hit Nick Appleyard in the back and killed him.

'Oh, no!' cried Richard. 'Appleyard is dead! Someone in the forest shot this black arrow.'

'Look! There's a message on the arrow,' said Hatch. 'What does it say, Richard?'

Richard took the arrow and read, '"*For Appleyard, from John, to make things right.*" What a strange message!'

'It's dangerous [2] here, let's go to the church,' said Hatch.

There were about twenty men on their horses outside the church. They were ready to fight.

'Sir Daniel will be pleased with these brave men,' said Hatch.

'Look at the church door,' said Richard. 'There's a letter on it!'

'A letter on the church door,' said Sir Oliver, surprised. He was the priest of the village and Sir Daniel's good friend. 'Young Richard, please read it.'

1. **mind** : 主意。　　　　　　2. **dangerous** : 危險的。

14

The Black Arrow

Richard took the letter off the door and read it aloud.

> *I have four black arrows.*
> *The first arrow killed Appleyard,*
> *the next one will kill Bennet Hatch,*
> *because he burnt Grimstone House.*
> *Another arrow is for Sir Oliver Oates,*
> *because he killed Sir Harry Shelton.*
> *Sir Daniel will get the fourth arrow.*
> *From John of the Green Wood and his men.*
> *P.S. Remember we have other arrows for your men!*

'We live in a terrible world! I'm a good man. I did not kill Sir Harry Shelton!' cried Sir Oliver Oates.

'We know you're a good, honest man, Sir Oliver,' said Hatch. Then he whispered [1] something in Sir Oliver's ear and looked at Richard. Sir Harry Shelton was Richard's father. Richard saw this but he said nothing.

'I must write a letter to Sir Daniel and tell him what happened,' said Sir Oliver.

When the letter was ready he said, 'Richard, take this important letter to Sir Daniel immediately. [2] Be careful on the road because it can be very dangerous.'

Richard took the letter and went to get his horse.

Hatch followed him. 'Richard,' he said quietly, 'you're a brave, honest young man. Listen to me, be careful of Sir Daniel. Don't trust him and don't trust Sir Oliver. They're dangerous men.'

Richard was surprised and started thinking. 'Thank you, my friend,' he said. Then he got on his grey horse and galloped [3] away.

---

1. **whispered** : 耳語；低聲説。
2. **immediately** : 馬上。
3. **galloped** : （騎馬）疾馳。

UNDERSTANDING THE TEXT

 COMPREHENSION CHECK

Are these sentences 'Right' (A) or 'Wrong' (B)? If there is not enough information to answer 'Right' (A) or 'Wrong' (B), choose 'Doesn't say' (C). There is an example at the beginning (0).

0   The bell is ringing because there will be a big battle soon.
    Ⓐ Right   B Wrong   C Doesn't say

1   Richard likes Sir Daniel.
    A Right   B Wrong   C Doesn't say

2   The people in the village are poor and unhappy.
    A Right   B Wrong   C Doesn't say

3   The women of the village don't want any more battles.
    A Right   B Wrong   C Doesn't say

4   Sir Daniel fights for the house of Lancaster.
    A Right   B Wrong   C Doesn't say

5   Nick Appleyard must go to Kettley to fight with Sir Daniel.
    A Right   B Wrong   C Doesn't say

6   Bennet Hatch kills Nick Appleyard.
    A Right   B Wrong   C Doesn't say

7   John of the Green Wood is an enemy of Sir Daniel and his friends.
    A Right   B Wrong   C Doesn't say

8   Sir Oliver Oates killed Richard's father, Sir Harry Shelton.
    A Right   B Wrong   C Doesn't say

2 VOCABULARY

Find adjectives （形容詞）for people and feelings in Chapter One that match these descriptions. The first letter is already there.

1   good-looking, but for a man   h _ _ _ _ _ _ _

2   in a very bad mood   a _ _ _ _

3   opposite of friendly   u _ _ _ _ _ _ _ _ _

4   not normal   s _ _ _ _ _ _

5   someone who's not afraid   b _ _ _ _

6   someone who tells the truth is…   h _ _ _ _ _

7   bad things can happen to you if a person
    or place is…   d _ _ _ _ _ _ _ _

8   if something happens, but you do not
    expect it, you are   s _ _ _ _ _ _ _ _

3 CHARACTERS

Match the people from the story to the correct descriptions.

1 ☐ Sir Oliver Oates   5 ☐ Nick Appleyard
2 ☐ Sir Daniel Brackley   6 ☐ Sir Harry Shelton
3 ☐ Richard Shelton   7 ☐ John of the Green Wood
4 ☐ Bennet Hatch

A   Richard's dead father.
B   A man who fights for Sir Daniel. Someone kills him with an arrow.
C   A priest and a friend of Sir Daniel's.
D   Sir Daniel's best friend.
E   His father is dead and Sir Daniel takes care of him.
F   He is angry with Sir Daniel and his friends. He wants to kill them.
G   He takes care of Richard, but people don't like him.

4 FILL IN THE GAPS

Here is the letter that Sir Oliver wrote to Sir Daniel. Use the words in the box to complete it.

arrow	battle	bell	Hatch	message	terrible
	three	twenty	villagers	ward	

Tunstall, 6 April 1468

Dear Sir Daniel,

I send you this letter with Richard, your (1) .... Things are not good here in Tunstall. We rang the castle (2) .... and sent a messenger to tell the men about the (3) .... in Kettley. But the (4) .... are not happy. The women are angry because they lose their husbands in the war. Only (5) .... brave men from the village will come to fight with you. I have more bad news.

A (6) .... thing happened today. Nick Appleyard was killed with a black (7) .... There was a (8) .... on the arrow. It said, 'From John'. Yes, my Lord, John of the Green Wood killed Nick. He says he has (9) .... more arrows. One for (10) ...., one for me and one for you.

Be careful, Sir Daniel. These are dangerous times!

Yours,

     Sir Oliver

BEFORE YOU READ

 VOCABULARY

Fill in the gaps in the paragraph below with words from the box.

> get   happy   good   money   wife
>   marry   husband   marriage

When two people (**1**) .... they become husband and
(**2**) .... Another way of saying 'to marry' is 'to (**3**) ....
married'. When two people get married, there is usually a special event,
called a wedding. The word (**4**) '...................' means the relationship
between (**5**) .... and wife. Now, when we talk about 'a
(**6**) .... marriage' we mean that two people are (**7**) ....
together, but in the past, when people talked about 'a good marriage',
they often meant it was good business: (**8**) .... was often more
important than love.

 READING PICTURES

**Look at the picture on page 23. It shows the inside of an inn, a place
where you can eat and drink and also stay the night.**

1   Look at the man sitting opposite Richard.

– How old do you think he is?

– Think of some adjectives to describe his physical appearance. If
necessary, use a dictionary or ask your teacher.

– Do you think he is a good character or a bad character? Why?

2   Look at the person behind Richard.

– Do you think it is a boy or a girl?

– Does the man sitting opposite Richard know that this person is
there?

 3   The person behind Richard is whispering (speaking very quietly) to
Richard. What do you think he/she is whispering? Make a guess, and
then read and/or listen to Chapter Two and find out!

A   He/she is asking for something to eat and drink.

B   He/she is asking for directions to go somewhere.

C   He/she is telling Richard the best things to eat.

D   He/she wants to know if he/she can leave with Richard.

E   He/she is trying to sell something to Richard.

CHAPTER TWO

John Matcham

S ir Daniel Brackley sat next to the fire at the Sign of the Sun Inn [1] in Kettley. He was a tall man of about forty. He was bald [2] and had a big nose and black eyes. He collected taxes all day and now he was thinking about how he could make more money. Sir Daniel was a very greedy [3] man and did many bad things.

A thin young boy was sitting near the door of the inn. He was very sad.

'Come here, John,' said Sir Daniel. The young boy was about thirteen, and had blond hair and blue eyes. He was wearing dirty, old clothes and a big brown hat.

Sir Daniel looked at him and laughed, 'You make me laugh, John!'

'Don't laugh at me!' said John angrily. 'I don't like it.'

'Oh, let me laugh!' said Sir Daniel. 'I'll plan a good marriage for you – you'll see.'

'And I'll make a lot of money with this marriage,' thought Sir Daniel. 'Lord Shoreby will pay me well...'

The young boy went to sit down again.

Some time later Richard came into the inn.

'Richard, my brave boy!' said Sir Daniel. 'Sit down and eat. You're probably hungry and thirsty.'

---

1. **inn** : 小酒店，客棧。
2. **bald** : 禿的。

3. **greedy** : 貪婪的。

'Here's an important letter from Sir Oliver,' said Richard, giving him the letter.

Sir Daniel read it and he was worried.

'Richard, the letter on the church door is a lie!'[1] said Sir Daniel. 'Sir Oliver did not kill your poor father. Ellis Duckworth killed your father, but he escaped[2] and we never found him.'

'Did this happen at Moat House Castle?' asked Richard, looking into Sir Daniel's eyes.

'It happened between Moat House and Holywood,' answered Sir Daniel. 'But now sit down and eat. I must answer Sir Oliver's letter and then you can take it back to him in Tunstall.'

While Richard was eating, he heard a soft voice near his ear.

'Please don't turn around,[3] but tell me the way to Holywood.'

'Take the road by the old church,' Richard whispered. He did not turn around but he saw the boy leave the inn quietly.

'Take this message to Tunstall immediately,' said Sir Daniel to Richard. Then he looked around the inn and said, 'Where is that girl – that boy, John?'

'He left the inn about an hour ago,' said Richard.

'I *must* find him!' cried Sir Daniel. He turned to one of his men and said, 'James, take six men and go and find that boy!'

Richard left the inn with the message. He rode his horse all night and early the next morning he was near a marsh.[4] In the marsh he saw a young boy on his horse, but the horse was not moving.

'You're the boy from the inn,' said Richard. 'I saw you last night.'

'Yes, I am,' he said. 'I'm lost and my horse hurt his leg in the marsh. Now he can't move.'

END

---

1. **lie** : 謊言。

2. **escaped** : 逃脫。

3. **turn around** : 轉身。

4. **marsh** : 沼澤。

'The poor horse!' said Richard. 'I'm sorry, but I must kill it. Please get off.' When the boy got off, he killed the horse.

'Can you help me go to Holywood, Master Shelton?' asked the boy.

'Yes, I can,' said Richard, 'but who are you?'

'Call me John Matcham,' said the boy.

'Why do you want to go to Holywood, John?' asked Richard.

'There's a kind friar [1] at Holywood and he'll protect me,' said John.

'Protect you?' asked Richard.

'Yes, he'll protect me from Sir Daniel Brackley,' said the boy. 'He's a very bad man. He took me from my home and gave me these dirty clothes to wear.'

'But I know Sir Daniel,' said Richard. 'He's not an evil [2] man.'

'He's evil and greedy, believe me,' said the boy. 'One day you'll understand why.' He was silent for a moment and then said, 'I heard that you are going to get married soon.'

'What?' said Richard laughing. 'And *who* am I going to marry?'

'Joanna Sedley,' said the boy. 'Sir Daniel planned the marriage.'

'Oh!' said Richard and his face became red. 'But I don't know her.'

Suddenly they heard a noise and saw Sir Daniel's seven men on the hill.

'Sir Daniel's men!' cried the boy. 'They're looking for me.'

'Don't worry, I'll take you to Holywood. I promise!' [3] said Richard. 'Get on my horse quickly.'

John smiled at his new friend and together they galloped into the dark forest.

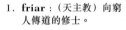

1. **friar**：（天主教）向窮
   人傳道的修士。

2. **evil**：邪惡的。
3. **promise**：承諾。

UNDERSTANDING THE TEXT

KET

1 COMPREHENSION CHECK

Choose the correct answer, A, B or C. There is an example at the beginning (0).

0   Sir Daniel spends his time
    A ☑ collecting money from villagers.
    B ☐ fighting battles.
    C ☐ drinking beer at the Sign of the Sun Inn.

1   Sir Daniel is planning a good marriage for John because
    A ☐ it will make John happy.
    B ☐ he will make a lot of money with it.
    C ☐ John is his only son.

2   Richard came to Kettley because
    A ☐ he had a letter to give to Sir Daniel.
    B ☐ he wanted to meet John.
    C ☐ he wanted to fight in the battle there.

3   When Richard's father died, Ellis Duckworth
    A ☐ went to prison.
    B ☐ was killed.
    C ☐ ran away.

4   John runs away to Holywood because
    A ☐ Sir Daniel has a castle there.
    B ☐ it is safe there.
    C ☐ Richard is going there.

5   Sir Daniel is planning a marriage for
    A ☐ John only.
    B ☐ John and Richard.
    C ☐ Richard only.

2 CHARACTERS

Read Chapter Two again. Which adjectives (形容詞) from the box best describe John Matcham, Sir Daniel Brackley and Richard Shelton?

bald	brave	evil	greedy	hungry	kind
	sad	thin	thirsty	worried	young

John Matcham : ....
Sir Daniel Brackley : ....
Richard Shelton : ....

③ GEOGRAPHY

The map shows places mentioned in Chapters One and Two. Match the letters from the map with the descriptions of each place.

1 ☐ Where John's horse got stuck
2 ☐ Where Sir Daniel is now
3 ☐ Where Sir Oliver found the letter
4 ☐ Where Nick was killed
5 ☐ Where Richard's father was killed
6 ☐ Where John wants to go to be safe

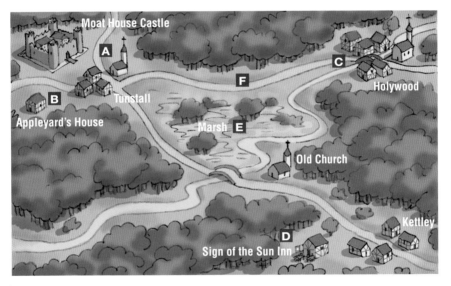

④ PREPOSITIONS

Complete this summary of Chapter Two with prepositions from the box.

about   on   for   from   from   in   to   with

Richard goes (1) .... his horse to Kettley. He has a letter (2) .... Sir Daniel. The letter has bad news and Sir Daniel is worried (3) .... what will happen.

At Kettley, Richard meets John Matcham. Sir Daniel took John (4) .... his home and is planning a marriage for him. John is sad, and escapes (5) .... Sir Daniel. He wants to go (6) .... Holywood, where a kind friar will protect him. John's horse gets stuck (7) .... a marsh, but Richard finds him and promises to go (8) .... him to Holywood.

BEFORE YOU READ

1 VOCABULARY

Match the first sentences (1-4) to those with a similar meaning (A-D).

1 ☐ For many years people from the same country fought with each other.

2 ☐ He will be the next king.

3 ☐ She will look after the children because their parents died.

4 ☐ This is the chair where the kings and queens sit.

A He's the **heir** to the throne.

B The children will be under her **guardianship**.

C There was a **civil war** for many years.

D This is the **throne**.

KET

2 LISTENING

Listen to the first part of the Wars of the Roses dossier and complete the fact file.

The Wars of the Roses	
When did it happen?	Between **(1)** .... and **(2)** ....
Who fought?	The **(3)** .... family and the **(4)** .... family
Why did they fight?	Because both wanted to be **(5)** ....
What were the family symbols?	A **(6)** .... and a **(7)** ....

The Wars of the Roses

There was civil[1] war in England from 1455 to 1485. This was because of an argument[2] between the families of York and Lancaster.

Each noble family at this time had a picture of an object which they used as a special symbol[3] of their family. The Lancastrians had a red rose and the Yorkists had a white rose. This gave the name to the Wars of the Roses.

Both the Yorkists and the Lancastrians were descendants[4]

The Lancastrian red rose.

The Yorkist white rose.

of King Edward III (1327-77) and both wanted to be king of England. END

In 1455 the king of England was Henry VI, a member of the Lancaster family. But the leader of the York family, John, Duke of York, also wanted to be king.

The first battle was in 1455 at St Albans, just north of London. The Yorkists won but Henry VI was still king. Three years passed before the next battle, but between 1459 and 1461 there were eight more battles. The Yorkists won five of these,

1. **civil** : 國內的。
2. **argument** : 爭執。
3. **symbol** : 標誌。
4. **descendants** : 後裔。

and finally, in 1461, there was a Yorkist king for the first time, Edward IV (1461-70, 1471-83).

After Edward IV's death in 1483, the heir [1] to the throne [2] was the eldest son, Edward V, but he was still a child at this time. Edward IV's brother, the Duke of Gloucester, was the guardian [3] of both the boy and his younger brother. The Duke also wanted to be king, so

The Princes Edward and Richard in the Tower (1878) by Sir John Everett Millais.

1. **heir** : 繼承人。
3. **guardian** : 監護人。
2. **throne** : 王位，王權。

Double portrait of Elizabeth of York and Henry VII holding the white rose of York and the red rose of Lancaster from "Memoirs of the Court of Queen Elizabeth" (1825).

he decided to put the boys in prison in the Tower of London. People believe that they were killed soon after their arrival and the Duke became King Richard III.

There were seventeen battles during the thirty years of war. These happened all over England: in the north, south, east and west. On 22 August 1485 Henry Tudor, a descendant of the house of Lancaster, won the final battle. Richard III, the last York king, was killed. Henry Tudor then became King Henry VII. A year later he married Elizabeth of York and the Lancaster and York families were joined together. To show this the white rose of York and the red rose of Lancaster became one red and white rose. This was called the Tudor Rose as was the symbol of the Tudors, a new line [1] of English kings and queens.

1. **line**：家系。

1 COMPREHENSION CHECK

Match the dates with the events.

1 ☐ Edward III dies.
2 ☐ Edward IV becomes king for the second time.
3 ☐ Duke of Gloucester puts Edward IV's sons in prison.
4 ☐ Henry VII marries Elizabeth of York.
5 ☐ House of York and House of Lancaster start fighting.
6 ☐ Last battle of the Wars of the Roses.

A 1377   B 1455   C 1471   D 1483   E 1485   F 1486

PROJECT ON THE WEB

Connect to the Internet and go to www.blackcat-cideb.com or www.cideb.it. Insert the title or part of the title of the book into our search engine. Open the page for *The Black Arrow*. Click on the Internet project link.

The Black Arrow was an important two-part TV serial in 1951.

Find out more about children's TV programmes of the 1950s.

Work with a friend and choose two programmes that interest you. Answer the following questions:

▶ What is the programme about?
▶ Who is the main character?
▶ Do you like him or her? Why?

Felix The Cat

'Felix the Cat'

In February 1956 ITV began to use some old Felix cartoons in a short series. The cat had been created by Otto Mesmer and developed by Pat Sullivan after Paramount had been interested enough in the original artwork to sign him up for the Paramount Screen Magazine. The first moving cartoon was made in 1919 and ...ical Mews, Felix was officially ...larity grew even greater in ... to survive the transition to ...ially due to the absence of a ...nation of punctuation marks.

POPEYE!

Was first presented on ITV in February 1958. The on-off love affair of Popeye and Olive ... munchin ... irritati ... series. ...

Popeye theme

Robin Hood (1953) - was a 30-minute serial in six parts written by Max Kester and based on the traditional medieval story. Patrick Troughton (*right*) starred as Robin, with Kenneth Mackintosh as Little John, Wensley Pithey as Friar Tuck, and David Kossoff as the Sheriff of Nottingham. The serial was produced by Joy Harington.

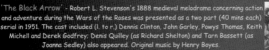

'The Black Arrow' - Robert L. Stevenson's 1888 medieval melodrama concerning action and adventure during the Wars of the Roses was presented as a two part (40 mins each) serial in 1951. The cast included (l. to r.) Dennis Clinton, John Garley, Powys Thomas, Keith Michell and Derek Godfrey; Denis Quilley (as Richard Shelton) and Tarn Bassett (as Joanna Sedley) also appeared. Original music by Henry Boyes.

'The Adventures of Sherlock Holmes' (1954-55) starred Ronald Howard as Sherlock Holmes, H. Marion Crawford as Dr. John Watson and Archie Duncan as Inspector Lestrade.

Theme

BEFORE YOU READ

1 VOCABULARY – A CASTLE

Look at the picture of the castle and use the words from the box to label it correctly.

1 ☐ moat   2 ☐ tower   3 ☐ drawbridge

4 ☐ stone wall   5 ☐ portcullis

2 READING PICTURES

Look at the picture on page 37. Work with a friend and take turns asking and answering these questions.

- Who is in the picture?
- Where are they?
- What are they doing?
- What's going to happen next?

3 LISTENING

Listen to the conversation and answer the questions.

1 Who is speaking? ....
2 What are they doing? ....
3 Where did Lawless get the eggs? ....
....
4 What does Lawless say about the Band of the Black Arrow?
....
5 What does Lawless hear? ....
6 Who do they think it is? ....

4 VOCABULARY

Use the words in the box to complete these questions.

attack	enemy	truth	leader	escape

1 Who is the .... of the Band of the Black Arrow?
2 Who is Sir Daniel's worst ....?
3 Who wants to .... Sir Daniel's men?
4 Who wants to .... from Sir Daniel's men?
5 Who wants to know the .... about his father?

Now read Chapter Three and answer the questions in exercise 4.

CHAPTER THREE

Moat House Castle

Richard and John rode through the dark forest of 🎧 Tunstall, where the tall trees moved in the wind. They stopped when they found a big, burnt [1] house.

'This house looks like Grimstone,' said Richard.

'Grimstone?' asked John. 'What's that?'

'It was Ellis Duckworth's house until Bennet Hatch burnt it down five years ago. It was a very beautiful house before the fire.'

Behind the house they saw some men sitting around a fire. They were wearing old, dark clothes and each man had a bow and arrow. They were eating and talking like old friends, and some were laughing.

Suddenly a man up a tall tree cried, 'I see seven of Sir Daniel's men coming here!'

'Is Sir Daniel with them?' asked a handsome man.

'No, I can't see him,' answered the man on the tall tree.

'Let's attack them!' cried the handsome man. 'Go to your places quickly!'

---

1. **burnt** : 燒壞的。

'I must go and tell Sir Daniel's men about the attack,' said Richard to John.

'But why?' asked John, surprised. 'They're looking for *me*! You promised to take me to Holywood. You can't leave me now!'

'You're right, John,' said Richard. 'I'll take you to Holywood.'

Richard remembered his promise. The men in the forest took their bows and arrows and ran to their places. They started attacking Sir Daniel's men.

When the attack was over one of the men in the forest saw Richard and wanted to kill him.

'No, don't!' cried the handsome man. It was Ellis Duckworth, the leader of the Band of the Black Arrow. 'This boy is Harry's son. We mustn't hurt him. Bring him to me immediately! I want to talk to him.'

Richard heard him and said, 'Oh, no! Let's run away from here, John! Quickly!'

The two boys ran to the top of a hill and two men followed them. John was tired but he continued running. They soon reached another forest and Richard said, 'No one is following us now – we're safe.'

'I can't walk or run anymore,' said John. 'I'm very tired.'

'Tired?' said Richard. 'What kind of a boy are you?'

John looked at him and started crying.

'Oh, please don't cry,' said Richard smiling. 'Look, there's a river. Let's go and drink some cold water.'

Later, when it was dark, they fell asleep under a tree.

The next morning they woke up and were hungry. But they had nothing to eat.

Suddenly they heard a noise coming from the forest. They saw

The Black Arrow

a friar walking towards them. His head was covered with a big hood. [1] He stopped near them and took off his hood.

'Sir Daniel!' cried Richard. 'This is a surprise! What are you doing here? And why are you dressed like a friar?'

'Richard,' said Sir Daniel, 'we lost the battle against York. It was a terrible battle and most of my men were killed. I am wearing friar's clothes so I can escape. Now I'm going home to Moat House Castle.'

Sir Daniel gave them both some bread and cheese. Richard and John ate quickly because they were very hungry.

'I'm surprised to see you two boys together,' said Sir Daniel. 'But now you're both coming with me, do you understand?'

'Very well, Sir Daniel,' said Richard.

'Yes, sir,' said John quietly.

Richard and John followed Sir Daniel and they soon arrived at the castle. Before going in John said, 'Well, Richard, now we must say goodbye.'

'But why?' said Richard. 'We're both going to Moat House Castle. We're good friends and we can see each other all the time.'

'You won't see me anymore,' said John sadly. 'And I can't explain why. I must do what Sir Daniel says. But remember, Richard, be careful of Sir Daniel.'

Richard did not like this mystery [2] and wanted to know more. 'Goodbye, my young friend,' said Richard sadly.

Moat House Castle was a stone castle with a drawbridge, a moat and four tall towers. There were now only twenty-two men

1. **hood** : 斗篷。　　　　　　　　　　2. **mystery** : 謎；難以理解的事物。

in the castle because a lot of them were killed during the last battle against York. These men were afraid of the Band of the Black Arrow because the band lived in the forest near the castle.

Richard went to his bedroom and closed the door. It was a big, cold room near the top of the castle. He did not have many things inside, just a large bed, a table and chair. Richard liked the room because it was somewhere he could stay on his own and think. Now he went to sit on the bed so he could think about all the recent [1] events.

'What's happening at Moat House Castle?' he thought. 'Why can't I see my friend John Matcham anymore? Why is everyone telling me to be careful of Sir Daniel? Who is Joanna Sedley? How can I marry her if I don't know her?'

Richard was very confused and looked out of the small window in his room. He could see the big forest and he started thinking about the letter from John of the Green Wood.

'The letter says Sir Oliver killed my father,' he thought. 'But Sir Daniel says the letter is not true. He says Ellis Duckworth killed him. Did Ellis Duckworth really kill him? I don't believe Sir Daniel because I think he's hiding [2] something from me. But what? I want to know the truth. I must know the truth and only Sir Daniel can answer my questions!'

1. **recent** : 最近的。　　　　　　　2. **hiding** : 隱瞞。

UNDERSTANDING THE TEXT

1 COMPREHENSION CHECK

When did these things happen? Put the events on the correct part of the time arrow. The first one is done for you.

the past ⟵─────────────────────────────

[ ]   **[F]**   [ ]   [ ]   [ ]   [ ]   [ ]

A Ellis Duckworth's men attack Sir Daniel's men.
B Richard and John escape and sleep in the forest.
C Sir Daniel takes Richard and John back to Moat House Castle.
D Richard and John meet Sir Daniel.
E Sir Daniel loses the battle at Kettley.
F Richard and John find Ellis Duckworth and his band.
G Ellis Duckworth's house is burnt down.

KET

2 COMPREHENSION CHECK

Are these sentences 'Right' (A) or 'Wrong' (B)? If there is not enough information to answer 'Right' (A) or 'Wrong' (B), choose 'Doesn't say' (C). There is an example at the beginning (0).

0 Bennet Hatch burnt down Ellis Duckworth's house.
   Ⓐ Right   B Wrong   C Doesn't say

1 The men behind the house are brothers.
   A Right   B Wrong   C Doesn't say

2 Richard wants to help the men.
   A Right   B Wrong   C Doesn't say

3 Richard decides to take John to Holywood.
   A Right   B Wrong   C Doesn't say

4 Ellis recognises Richard.
   A Right   B Wrong   C Doesn't say

5 John can't walk because he has a broken leg.
   A Right   B Wrong   C Doesn't say

6 Sir Daniel was hurt during the battle at Kettley.
   A Right   B Wrong   C Doesn't say

7 Richard and John will share a room in Moat House Castle.
   A Right   B Wrong   C Doesn't say

8 Richard doesn't trust Sir Daniel.
   A Right   B Wrong   C Doesn't say

3 ▸ CONVERSATION

What does Richard say to Sir Daniel? Complete the conversation. Choose the right answers (A-H) to the questions (1-5). There are more answers than you need. There is an example at the beginning (0).

0	Where did you find John?	...E....
1	Where did you go then?	....
2	Who was there?	....
3	Was he alone?	....
4	What happened while you were there?	....
5	Then what did you do?	....

A   No. He was with his men.

B   Yes, it was.

C   Some of your men came, and there was a fight.

D   We ran away from Duckworth's house and then you found us.

E   I found him at the marsh, near the old church.

F   No, we didn't go.

G   We went through the forest until we came to Ellis Duckworth's house.

H   Ellis Duckworth.

4 ▸ ARTICLES

Complete the paragraph with *a*, *an* or *the* or '_' if no word is necessary.

Richard and John rode through (**1**) .... forest. They found (**2**) .... house. The house was burnt down and Richard said it was (**3**) .... Ellis Duckworth's house. They saw (**4**) .... group of men behind (**5**) .... house. They were sitting around (**6**) .... fire. It was (**7**) .... Band of the Black Arrow.

A man up in (**8**) .... oak tree told (**9**) .... others that (**10**) .... group of Sir Daniel's men were coming. Every man took (**11**) .... arrow and hid. They got ready to make (**12**) .... attack on Sir Daniel's men. Who should Richard help – Sir Daniel's men or John? It was (**13**) .... difficult decision.

When Richard heard (**14**) .... man say his father's name, he decided to run. Richard and John ran until John couldn't run anymore. That night they slept near (**15**) .... river. The next day they saw a friar walking towards them. When he took off his hood, they saw that (**16**) .... friar was Sir Daniel.

BEFORE YOU READ

1 WORD GAME

In this chapter, Richard wants to know what's true and what isn't.
Complete the crossword with words related to 'the truth'. The letters of
each word are after the clues... in the wrong order!

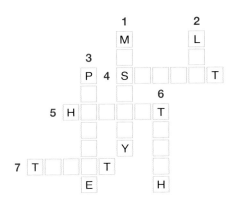

1   Richard wants to solve the .... about his father. [isytmyers]
2   What Sir Daniel told Richard about his father's death not the truth, it
    is a .... [ile]
3   Richard made a .... to John. [oiermsp]
4   John knows a .... about Richard. [ctrese]
5   Sir Daniel is not an .... man. [oethns]
6   Is Sir Daniel telling the ....? [rthtu]
7   Richard doesn't .... Sir Daniel. [srtut]

2 LISTENING

Listen to the beginning of Chapter Four and answer these questions.

1   Where is Richard?
    ....
2   How is he feeling?
    ....
3   What questions does he want to ask? Prepare three questions.
    ....

Joanna Sedley

Someone knocked on Richard's door. It was Bennet Hatch.

'Good afternoon, Richard,' he said, 'Sir Daniel wants to see you immediately.'

'Good!' said Richard. 'I want to see him too. I have a lot of things to ask him. There are too many mysteries at Moat House Castle – too many things I don't understand. Sir Daniel is not telling me the truth.'

'Richard,' said Hatch, 'please be careful. Don't ask Sir Daniel certain questions…'

'What do you mean, Hatch?' asked Richard.

'Well, you know… certain questions about…'

'I want answers to my questions!' said Richard angrily, and he went to Sir Daniel's room. Sir Oliver was there. He was sitting in a corner of the room and his face was white.

'Come in, Richard,' said Sir Daniel. 'Please sit down. You look worried, my boy. Are you still thinking about that letter on the church door?'

'Yes, and I want some answers,' said Richard. 'My father was killed when I was a little boy. People say that you and Sir Oliver killed him. I want to know the truth.'

END

'Oh Richard, do you really think I killed your father?' said Sir Daniel, smiling. 'Your father was my friend. When he died I looked after you all these years and taught you many things. And poor Sir Oliver! He's a priest – a kind, honest man.'

'Sir Daniel, for many years you used my family's money because I live with you,' said Richard angrily. 'And you'll soon plan my marriage and get a lot of money for it!'

'How can you say these terrible things?' cried Sir Daniel. 'You're making me very angry! But you're still a boy! We'll talk about this when you're a man. Remember, I did not kill your father – I promise.'

When Sir Oliver heard the words 'I promise' he jumped in his chair. Richard saw this and understood a lot.

After he left the room Sir Daniel said, 'The boy asks too many questions – he knows too many things. Put him in the room above the church!'

'The room above the church?' asked Sir Oliver quietly.

'Yes, you heard me!' said Sir Daniel.

Richard went to his room and remembered Hatch's words: 'Don't trust Sir Daniel or Sir Oliver.'

In the evening one of Sir Daniel's men came to his room and said, 'Follow me, Master Shelton, you'll sleep in another room tonight.'

'In another room?' asked Richard.

'Yes, in the room above the church,' said the man. 'It's nice and big… but it's full of ghosts!'

'Full of ghosts?' thought Richard. 'What does he mean?'

Richard sat on the big bed in the new room and he was worried. He did not know that many men were killed in that room.

'I must leave this castle immediately,' he thought. 'Something bad is happening.'

Suddenly someone knocked on the door. It was John Matcham.

'John! I'm happy to see you,' said Richard.

'Oh, Richard, listen to me!' said John. 'I heard Sir Daniel's men talking. They want to kill you! I want to help you escape. I think there's a secret way out of this room.'

They started looking for it and found a small trapdoor [1] under a table.

'This is the secret way out!' said John excitedly. 'We can escape together.'

Then they heard Sir Daniel's voice: 'Joanna! Joanna, where are you?'

'Who is Joanna?' asked Richard.

John looked at Richard and said, 'I am Joanna!'

'You!' said Richard, surprised. 'Then you're not a boy – you're a girl. You're Joanna Sedley!'

'Yes, I'm Joanna Sedley!' She took off her big hat and Richard could see her long blonde hair. She was very pretty.

'You're a brave girl!' said Richard smiling. 'And you're beautiful, too!'

They could hear Sir Daniel's voice again: 'Joanna, where are you?'

'We must escape immediately!' said Joanna.

---

1. **trapdoor** : 地板門。

They opened the trapdoor and went down the long secret corridor. [1] They came to a big door but it was locked.

'What can we do now?' asked Joanna.

'I don't know,' said Richard. 'Perhaps someone will open this door because we're near the church. Let's wait here.'

They sat down on the stone floor.

'Are you Sir Daniel's ward too?' asked Richard.

'Yes, my mother and father are dead and my family was rich. At first Lord Foxham looked after me; he was a good man. Then Sir Daniel took me. After some time Lord Foxham took me back. He wanted me to marry Lord Hamley. When Sir Daniel heard this he decided to kidnap [2] me! He gave me these boy's clothes and said, "You will marry Richard Shelton." Every marriage brings Sir Daniel a lot of money.'

'I'm happy I met you, Joanna!' said Richard.

'I am too,' she said.

Suddenly they realised [3] someone was behind them. It was Bennet Hatch.

'Hatch, what are you doing here?' asked Richard, surprised.

'I'm looking for you, Richard,' said Hatch. 'Sir Daniel wants to kill you, but not Joanna. I want to help you both escape. Here is the key to the door.'

He took an old key from his pocket and opened the big door. 'Now you can escape across the church to the tower. I'll tell Sir Daniel I couldn't find you. Good luck!'

1. **corridor** : 通道。
2. **kidnap** : 綁架。
3. **realised** : 意識到。

UNDERSTANDING THE TEXT

① SUMMARY
Read this summary of Chapter Four and find six mistakes.

Richard and John are now at Moat House Castle. Richard has a lot of questions. For example, he wants to know who killed his brother. Bennet Hatch tells Richard to be careful. He also tells him not to trust John Matcham.

Richard and Sir Daniel argue. Sir Daniel thinks Richard knows too much. That evening, some men take Richard to the room above the old theatre. They tell him it's full of mice!

John comes to Richard's room. He takes off his hat, and Richard understands that John is really a girl! Her name is Joanna Sedley. They find a secret trapdoor under the bed. Bennet Hatch finds them. He doesn't help them to escape.

② CHARACTERS
Who said what? Match the character with things they said.

1 ☐ Bennet Hatch   2 ☐ Sir Oliver   3 ☐ Richard

4 ☐ Joanna Sedley   5 ☐ Sir Daniel   6 ☐ Sir Daniel's man

A   'People aren't telling me the truth.'
B   'I must kill him. He knows too much.'
C   'I'm not what I seem to be.'
D   'I did something very bad and now I'm afraid.'
E   'I must help Richard and Joanna.'
F   'Follow me, Master Shelton, you'll sleep in another room tonight.'

KET

LISTENING

Listen to Richard talking to Joanna and choose the correct answer, A, B or C.

1 How old was Joanna when her parents died?
   A ☐ 12
   B ☐ 13
   C ☐ 15

2 How did they die?
   A ☐ In a road accident.
   B ☐ In a fire.
   C ☐ They became ill.

3 Who lived at Crombey Hall?
   A ☐ Lord Foxham.
   B ☐ Joanna and her parents.
   C ☐ Sir Oliver.

4 Who was Lord Foxham?
   A ☐ A friend of Joanna's father.
   B ☐ A friend of Sir Daniel.
   C ☐ A neighbour.

5 Why did Joanna go to Moat House Castle?
   A ☐ Because she was kidnapped by Sir Oliver.
   B ☐ Because she wanted to meet Lord Hamley.
   C ☐ Because she was invited to a party.

6 Why did Foxham want Joanna to marry Hamley?
   A ☐ Because he thought she would be happy.
   B ☐ Because Hamley was very rich.
   C ☐ Because Hamley was the same age as Joanna.

7 Why didn't she want to marry Hamley?
   A ☐ He wasn't very rich.
   B ☐ He was a cruel man.
   C ☐ He was very old.

8 Where was Joanna when Sir Daniel kidnapped her?
   A ☐ In her bedroom.
   B ☐ In the garden.
   C ☐ In the kitchen.

50

KET

4 VOCABULARY

**Can you find words in Chapter Four that match these descriptions?
The first letter is already there.**

1 What you find in a haunted house!   g _ _ _ _
2 A small, secret door   t _ _ _ _ _ _ _
3 A passage inside a building   c _ _ _ _ _ _ _
4 To take someone away by force   k _ _ _ _ _
5 A very tall building   t _ _ _ _

BEFORE YOU READ

1 VOCABULARY

Write the correct word from the box under each picture.

rope   prisoner   stone

 [_____] **2** [_____] **3** [_____]

2 LISTENING

 **Listen to the beginning of Chapter Five. Then match the two halves of
the sentences below.**

1 ☐ If they reach the forest...   A ...they will be prisoners again.
2 ☐ If the rope breaks...   B ...they will be free.
3 ☐ If Sir Daniel's men see them...   C ...they will fall into the moat.

What do you think will happen?

CHAPTER FIVE

Ellis Duckworth

ichard and Joanna ran across the church to the castle tower. Richard tied the rope around a big stone. He looked back and saw no one.

'We must climb down the tower to the moat and swim to the other side,' he said. 'Then we can run to the forest and we'll be free.'

'Very well,' said Joanna bravely.

'I'll go first and you can follow me,' said Richard. 'Can you climb down a rope, Joanna?'

'I'll try!' she said.

Richard started climbing down the rope. One of Sir Daniel's men on the other tower saw him.

'Shelton's trying to escape!' he shouted. He shot Richard in the arm with an arrow. Richard fell into the moat and tried to swim to the other side. Arrows were flying from the tower into the moat.

When Joanna saw Richard falling into the moat, she screamed. [1] One of Sir Daniel's men heard her and took her by the arm. She was Sir Daniel's prisoner [2] again!

END

---

1. **screamed** : 尖叫。
2. **prisoner** : 囚犯。

Richard got out of the water and ran into the forest. From there he could see Moat House Castle, but he could not see Joanna.

'One of Sir Daniel's men probably caught her,' he thought. 'But Sir Daniel won't hurt her because he wants to plan her marriage. I'll come back and rescue [1] her soon.'

His arm hurt and he could not walk. He fell to the ground on the leaves.

Ellis Duckworth and another man found Richard the next morning. He was very ill, so they took him to an inn and put him to bed.

When Richard woke up he said, 'Oh, my arm and head hurt a lot!'

Ellis Duckworth took his hand and smiled, 'My dear boy, I'm Ellis Duckworth and I was your father's best friend. He was like a brother to me.'

He looked at the other man and said, 'He's Lawless, one of my best men. Now Richard, please sleep. When you're better you'll tell me your story and we'll help you.'

The next day Richard was feeling better and he told Ellis Duckworth his long story.

'I'm happy you're here with us,' said Ellis. 'We're the Band of the Black Arrow, and we want to punish [2] bad people. I know you're brave and loyal, Richard. Together we'll fight and destroy [3] Sir Daniel! And we'll rescue Joanna, too! But first we must find out where she is.'

A few days later a mysterious messenger took this letter to Moat House Castle.

---

1. **rescue** : 營救。
2. **punish** : 懲罰。

3. **destroy** : 摧毀。

The Black Arrow

> *To Sir Daniel Brackley,*
> *You are a bad man; you are greedy and dishonest. Now I know*
> *you killed my father. One day I will kill you.*
> *Leave Joanna Sedley alone! I want to marry her soon.*
> *Richard Shelton*

Sir Daniel read the letter and thought, 'That boy is dangerous. I must find him.'

Many months passed and it was already winter. The house of Lancaster won a lot of battles and became strong and important. York was very weak now.

The town of Shoreby-on-the-Till was full of Lancaster nobles: [1] Sir Daniel with sixty men, his friend Lord Shoreby with two hundred men, and many others.

One cold winter night in January three men of the Band of the Black Arrow sat in a dark inn.

'I don't like this place,' said one man. 'There are too many enemies here.'

'We're here to help Master Shelton,' said Lawless.

Suddenly a young man came into the inn. 'Master Shelton,' said Lawless, 'Sir Daniel left the inn a few minutes ago with six men.'

'Let's follow him,' said Richard. It was dark outside, but they could see Sir Daniel and his men walking towards the sea.

Near the sea they saw an old lord [2] with some men. He was short and fat. He met Sir Daniel in front of a stone house with a wall around it.

Richard and his men hid behind some trees and watched the two men. But they could not hear them speak.

'It's old Lord Shoreby!' thought Richard angrily. 'He's another greedy man.'

---

1. **nobles** : 貴族。　　　　　　　2. **lord** : 貴族，領主。

'Tell me, Sir Daniel, how is the young girl?' asked the old lord. 'Is she very beautiful?'

'Lord Shoreby,' said Sir Daniel, 'Joanna Sedley's young, beautiful and... very rich. She'll be an excellent wife. The Sedley family was very rich and very important. She'll bring you a lot of money.'

'And I'll pay *you* a lot of money, Sir Daniel, but I want to see her now,' said Lord Shoreby.

Sir Daniel and Lord Shoreby went into the stone house followed by their men. When they came out, Lord Shoreby was smiling and went home. Sir Daniel and his men went back to the inn.

'Now we know Joanna is Sir Daniel's prisoner,' said Richard. 'And Lord Shoreby wants to marry her – that greedy old man! We must stop this marriage! I want to look inside of the house. Lawless, come with me, please. The others can wait here.'

Richard climbed to the top of the stone wall. From there he could see the kitchen window and Joanna. She was sitting at a table with Bennet Hatch's wife, and three of Sir Daniel's men stood behind her.

'She's very beautiful,' thought Richard. He was happy to see her, but he was angry with Sir Daniel and Lord Shoreby. He climbed down the wall and said to his men, 'I saw Joanna; she's inside. We must rescue her. Let's think of a good plan!'

UNDERSTANDING THE TEXT

1 COMPREHENSION CHECK

Choose the correct answer, A, B or C. There is an example at the beginning (0).

0 They tie the rope to a stone and then
- A ✓ Richard climbs down.
- B ☐ Joanna climbs down.
- C ☐ they climb down together.

1 One of Sir Daniel's men shoots
- A ☐ Joanna in the arm.
- B ☐ Richard in the arm.
- C ☐ Richard in the leg.

2 Ellis Duckworth finds Richard
- A ☐ in the forest.
- B ☐ in the moat.
- C ☐ near the inn.

3 The letter to Sir Daniel is from
- A ☐ Ellis Duckworth.
- B ☐ Richard Shelton.
- C ☐ Lord Shoreby.

4 Joanna is a prisoner in
- A ☐ Moat House Castle.
- B ☐ an inn in the town of Shoreby-on-the-Till.
- C ☐ a stone house by the sea.

5 Ellis decides to help Richard because
- A ☐ he loves Joanna.
- B ☐ he'll make money.
- C ☐ he hates Sir Daniel.

6 The two men that Richard sees talking are
- A ☐ Sir Daniel and Lord Shoreby.
- B ☐ Lord Shoreby and Sir Oliver.
- C ☐ Lord Shoreby and Master Shelton.

7 Lord Shoreby and Richard Shelton
- A ☐ meet in the inn.
- B ☐ both want to marry Joanna.
- C ☐ are both friends of Ellis Duckworth.

8 Richard sees Joanna
- A ☐ with Lord Shoreby.
- B ☐ with Bennet Hatch's wife.
- C ☐ alone.

WORD GAME – CHARACTERS

Underline all the adjectives（形容詞）that describe people in Chapter Five. Then try to find 13 adjectives in the word search square.

```
B E A U T I F U L S
D R D F C D E D G T
G A A Y O U N G R L
R G N V V G E O I O
E W G G E B H M C Y
E M R R E S T N H A
D L Y Y B R I R X L
Y O O K A P O V Z F
J L Q U D S O U A A
G D I S H O N E S T
```

Now match the adjectives to the characters.

....
....

 A SECRET MESSAGE

Here is a secret message that Joanna gave to the mysterious messenger. Break the code and find out who the message is for and what it says.

Efbs Sjdibse

J bn b qsjtpofs jo b iptf ofbs uif tfb. Csbdlmfz xbout nf up nbssz Tipsfcz. Qmfbtf sftdvf nf. Cf dbsfgvm, nz mpwf. Csbdlmfz jt ebohfspvt.

Kpboob

Clue: b = a, f = e, j = i

Now write your own secret message using the same code. Give your message to your best friend.

58

BEFORE YOU READ

1 VOCABULARY – DESCRIPTIONS
Can you match the pictures with the people?

acrobat   friar   merchant   musician   soldier   lord

1 _____

2 _____

3 _____

4 _____

5 _____

6 _____

Now match the same people with these descriptions.

1 A religious man. He usually lives with others in a monastery.
....

2 A man or woman in the army.
....

3 Someone who buys and sells things.
....

4 Someone who plays a musical instrument.
....

5 An entertainer who does incredible tricks with his or her body.
....

6 A man who has a high position in society.
....

CHAPTER SIX

The Two Friars

Richard and the men of the Black Arrow decided to attack Sir Daniel's house near the sea and rescue Joanna.

That night Richard and his twenty men climbed over the wall of the house. But Sir Daniel's men attacked them before they could get into the house. Sir Daniel had sixty men and Richard had only twenty. His men fought bravely, but they could not get into the house and rescue Joanna. Many men were hurt and some were killed. They went back to the forest.

When Sir Daniel heard about the attack he said, 'Shelton wants to rescue Joanna and marry her. We must take her to my castle in Shoreby. She'll be safe there and she'll marry Lord Shoreby in a few days.'

The next morning Richard and Lawless sat by the fire.

'If we don't rescue Joanna, she'll have to marry that old lord,' said Richard sadly. 'What can we do?'

Lawless looked at him and said, 'Perhaps I can help you. Follow me.'

'Where are we going?' asked Richard.

'To a secret place,' said Lawless.

They walked in the snow to a small den [1] under a big tree. Inside the den there was a table and a wooden box.

'This is my secret den,' said Lawless.

'Your secret den!' said Richard, surprised. 'It's very small.'

Lawless opened the wooden box and took out a friar's robe. [2] It was old and brown. Then he took out another one.

'What are these?' asked Richard.

'They're two friar's robes. Let's put them on and everyone will think we're friars.'

'But why?' asked Richard, confused.

'With these robes no one will recognise us!' said Lawless. 'We can easily get into Sir Daniel's castle in Shoreby. Remember, no one stops a friar.'

'Sir Daniel's castle in Shoreby – but why?' asked Richard.

'Master Shelton!' cried Lawless. 'Joanna is now in his castle and she'll soon marry old Lord Shoreby! Now do you understand?'

Richard was very surprised.

'How do you know this?' he asked.

'Young man, I'm Lawless… and I'm much older than you. I know a lot of things you don't know.'

'But how can we stop this marriage?' asked Richard.

1. **den** : 洞穴。

2. **friar's robe** : 修士袍。

'We'll think of a plan,' said Lawless. 'Now put on the friar's robe.'

Richard put on the robe and asked, 'How do I look?'

'Not bad, but I must do something to your face now,' answered Lawless.

He took some dark pencils from the box and drew a moustache and a small beard [1] on Richard's young face.

'Perfect!' he said. 'Now you look like a friar. Remember to keep your hood on and no one will recognise you.'

Lawless put on the other robe and they left the den.

When they got to Shoreby they went to the castle. There were a lot of people at the castle: rich gentlemen with their ladies, soldiers, merchants, musicians and acrobats.

The two friars went to a soldier and said, 'We're here to visit Joanna Sedley.'

'Her room is on the second floor,' said the soldier.

The two friars went to the second floor and found Joanna's room.

'I'll wait outside,' said Lawless.

Richard entered Joanna's room and took off his hood.

'Joanna!' he said softly. 'It's me, Richard.'

She ran to him and they hugged. [2]

'Oh, Richard,' Joanna said, 'I'm happy to see you! What are you doing here?'

'I'm here with a friend to rescue you,' said Richard.

'But how?' Joanna asked. 'I'm Sir Daniel's prisoner and I have to marry Lord Shoreby tomorrow morning! I'm so unhappy because I don't want to marry him.'

1. **moustache and a small beard :**

2. **hugged :**

The Black Arrow

'You won't marry that horrible [1] old man!' said Richard. 'I promise, Joanna. I want to marry you.'

He put on his hood and left the room quietly. He and Lawless went to the church to think of a plan. But Richard met Sir Oliver in the church.

'Richard Shelton!' he said, surprised. 'Sir Daniel is looking for you. You're in great danger.'

'I'm here to stop Joanna's marriage,' said Richard. 'I'm not afraid of Sir Daniel.'

'You can't stop this marriage,' said the priest, 'because Sir Daniel will kill you. You must stay in this church until tomorrow morning and then leave. If you try to escape, I'll call the soldiers.'

Richard and Lawless could not move.

At nine o'clock the next morning there were a lot of people in the church. Richard and Lawless were there, too. Joanna was wearing a beautiful white dress and had flowers in her head. But she was pale [2] and sad. Old Lord Shoreby was wearing his best clothes.

Joanna and Lord Shoreby stood in front of the priest. Ellis Duckworth and his men were hiding on the stairs of the church tower. Suddenly a black arrow flew across the church and killed Lord Shoreby!

Joanna and the people in the church screamed. Sir Daniel and his men took Joanna away immediately. Richard and Lawless were angry but they could do nothing. They watched Joanna leave with Sir Daniel.

---

1. **horrible** : 可怕的。

2. **pale** : 面色蒼白的。

UNDERSTANDING THE TEXT

1 COMPREHENSION CHECK

Are these sentences 'Right' (A) or 'Wrong' (B)? If there is not enough information to answer 'Right' (A) or 'Wrong' (B), choose 'Doesn't say' (C). There is an example at the beginning (0).

0 Richard is injured in the fight at the house near the sea.
  A Right   B Wrong   Ⓒ Doesn't say

1 Richard didn't rescue Joanna.
  A Right   B Wrong   C Doesn't say

2 Sir Daniel has more than one castle.
  A Right   B Wrong   C Doesn't say

3 It was now summer.
  A Right   B Wrong   C Doesn't say

4 Lawless has lots of different costumes in his den.
  A Right   B Wrong   C Doesn't say

5 In those days, friars could go anywhere they wanted.
  A Right   B Wrong   C Doesn't say

6 Richard is younger than Lawless.
  A Right   B Wrong   C Doesn't say

7 When they arrived at the castle, no one was there.
  A Right   B Wrong   C Doesn't say

8 Ellis Duckworth shot Lord Shoreby.
  A Right   B Wrong   C Doesn't say

2 SUMMARY

Match the beginnings (1-8) with the endings (A-H) to make a summary of Chapter Six.

1 ☐ Richard and his men attack the house,
2 ☐ Sir Daniel hides Joanna at
3 ☐ Lawless thinks of a plan to
4 ☐ Lawless and Richard dress as Friars because
5 ☐ Richard and Lawless get into the castle and
6 ☐ They go to the church to think of a plan, but
7 ☐ The next day everyone is in the church because
8 ☐ Suddenly a black arrow

A   but they cannot rescue Joanna.
B   get inside the castle at Shoreby.
C   his castle in Shoreby.
D   kills Lord Shoreby, but Sir Daniel takes Joanna away.
E   Lord Shoreby will marry Joanna.
F   on the way they meet Sir Oliver.
G   they can go anywhere they want.
H   they find Joanna.

3 WORD GAME
Complete the crossword with words from Chapter Six.

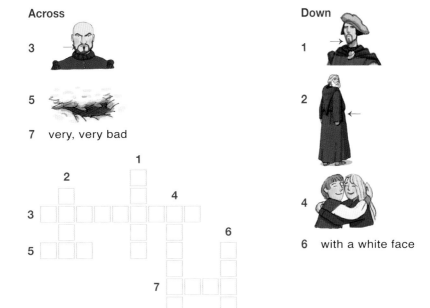

Across

3

5

7   very, very bad

Down

1

2

4

6   with a white face

T: GRADE 4

4 SPEAKING: SEASONAL ACTIVITIES
Richard and Lawless walked in the snow. Talk to your best friend about the activities you like doing in different seasons. Use these questions to help you.

1   What do you like doing in winter?
2   What do you like doing on the beach in summer?
3   Do you prefer autumn or spring? Why?

⑤ FILL IN THE GAPS

Complete Sir Oliver's diary with the Past Simple form（簡單過去式）of these verbs（動詞）.

be	can	come	go	meet	put	see	tell

Sunday, 28 January 1469

Last night I (1) .... to the castle church and I (2) .... not believe my eyes! I (3) .... Richard Shelton. He (4) .... with one of Ellis Duckworth's men. They plan to rescue Joanna. I (5) .... them that Sir Daniel will kill them if they try. I (6) .... them in the church and locked the door. Thankfully, nobody (7) .... us. I (8) .... straight back to my room. Tomorrow Shoreby will marry the girl and it will be too late for Shelton.

BEFORE YOU READ

KET

① NOTICES

Which notice (A-E) says this (1-5). For questions 1-5 mark the correct letter A-E.

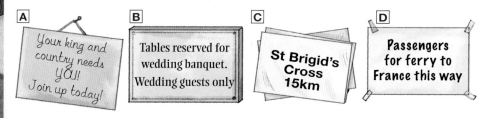

A	B	C	D
Your king and country needs you!! Join up today!	Tables reserved for wedding banquet. Wedding guests only	St Brigid's Cross 15km	Passengers for ferry to France this way

1 ☐ A famous battle took place here.
2 ☐ Become a soldier to help your county.
3 ☐ Follow this route to find your transport.
4 ☐ Only wedding guests can sit here.
5 ☐ This town is 15 kilometres away.

Historical Site
Battle of Shoreby
Castle, 1469

E

What do you think is the connection between these signs and the next chapter?

CHAPTER SEVEN

The Victory of York

ichard and Lawless returned to the forest. That
night Ellis Duckworth's men sat around the fire.

'There's going to be an important battle tomorrow
between the houses of Lancaster and York,' said
Duckworth to his men. 'We're going to attack
Shoreby Castle. This time York will win!'

'Hurrah!' cried the men.

'And we're going to find my enemy, Sir Daniel. Remember,
there's a black arrow waiting for him and his good friends, Bennet
Hatch and Sir Oliver Oates!'

'We'll find them!' cried the men.

'Richard,' said Duckworth, 'go and meet the Duke of
Gloucester at St Brigid's Cross tomorrow morning. Take him this
important message:'

Dear Richard, Duke of Gloucester,
My twenty men will meet your soldiers outside Shoreby Castle
before the battle. We will fight together and win!
Ellis Duckworth

Very early the next morning Richard rode to St Brigid's Cross.
It was a cold morning and there was a lot of snow on the road.
When he got there he saw a young knight dressed in armour [1] on
a big black horse. The white rose of the house of York was on his

---

1. **armour** : 盔甲。

shield. He was alone and he was fighting eight soldiers. He was a good fighter and killed three soldiers.

'I can help you, sir,' cried Richard. He and the knight fought together and the fight was soon over.

The young knight was surprised. He turned to Richard and said, 'Thank you for your help. You're a good fighter and you saved my life! Who are you?'

'I'm Richard Shelton and I'm looking for the Duke of Gloucester.'

'Well, you found him!' said the knight. 'I'm Richard, Duke of Gloucester.'

'Here's a message from Ellis Duckworth,' said Richard, giving him the letter.

The Duke read the letter and said, 'Good! I need more brave men for this battle. Duckworth is a loyal friend and together we'll win.'

Soon the Duke's soldiers arrived. They were carrying flags with the white rose of York.

'We're ready,' he cried. 'Let's attack Shoreby Castle!'

Many of the soldiers at Shoreby Castle were still sleeping when the Duke attacked. Hundreds of soldiers fought in a long battle and many were killed. At the end of the battle there was a fire and Shoreby Castle was almost destroyed. The house of York won the battle and Sir Daniel escaped with Joanna, Bennet Hatch and two men.

The Duke of Gloucester was pleased with the victory. He went to Richard and said, 'You're a brave young man and you fought well. Kneel down, [1] Richard, I want to knight [2] you!'

Richard knelt down in front of the Duke and became 'Sir Richard'. This was a great honour for him.

1. **Kneel down** :   2. **to knight** : 封爵，授爵。

The next day Sir Richard left Shoreby and started looking for Joanna. He knew she was with Sir Daniel. He travelled all day and in the evening he saw a small fire on a hill.

'Perhaps that's Sir Daniel's fire,' he thought. He moved silently through the trees and got closer. He saw Sir Daniel, Bennet Hatch and a young boy sitting near the fire. They were eating and talking.

'Joanna is dressed as John Matcham again!' thought Richard. 'Sir Daniel is very clever!'

Richard hid behind a big tree and watched them. It was obvious [1] that Joanna was very sad.

He waited until they were finally asleep and then he quietly went up to Joanna.

'Joanna,' he whispered in her ear, 'wake up.'

She woke up and smiled.

'We must be very quiet,' whispered Sir Richard. 'Get up slowly and follow me.'

They moved away very quietly through the trees.

They got on Sir Richard's horse and went into the forest. That night they slept at Ellis Duckworth's camp [2] near Holywood.

When Joanna woke up she said, 'This is like a dream, Richard. We're together again!'

'Yes, and tomorrow we can get married!' Sir Richard said excitedly. 'I'm going to talk to the kind friar of Holywood Abbey this morning.'

'I'm very happy, Richard!' said Joanna.

Sir Richard woke up very early on the day of his marriage. He was the happiest man in the world.

He put on his best clothes and took a short walk in the forest.

---

1. **obvious** : 明顯的。　　　　　　　2. **camp** : 營地。

Soon he saw a friar walking towards him. As the friar came closer he recognised him – it was Sir Daniel! He put his hand on his sword because he was ready to fight.

'I'm not here to fight you,' said Sir Daniel sadly. 'My men and I fought bravely, but we lost the battle against the house of York. It was a long, terrible battle. And now I have nothing! I lost my castle, my men, my money, my jewels... [1] I lost everything. Now I must escape to France where I still have some friends. I hope they can help me.'

'Go to France, Sir Daniel, and don't come back!' said Sir Richard angrily.

Sir Daniel turned around and continued walking in the forest. But after a minute a black arrow flew through the morning air and hit him in the heart. He fell to the ground and Sir Richard ran to his side.

'Richard,' he said quietly. 'Is the arrow... black?'

'Yes, it's black,' said Richard.

Sir Daniel looked at him for the last time and died.

'I killed him,' said a voice in the forest. It was Ellis Duckworth. 'And yesterday I killed Bennet Hatch.' He walked out of the forest and stood by Richard.

'You killed all of your enemies except one,' said Richard.

'Yes, Sir Oliver is still alive,' said Duckworth.

'Don't kill him, Ellis,' said Richard. 'Let's live in peace.'

Duckworth thought for a moment. He looked at the body of Sir Daniel and said, 'You're right, Richard, I want to live in peace. I don't want to fight or kill anymore. The Band of the Black Arrow doesn't exist anymore.'

1. **jewels** : 珠寶。

The Black Arrow

At nine o'clock that morning Richard and Joanna finally got married at Holywood Abbey. [1] It was a beautiful wedding and everyone was happy. Richard, Joanna, Ellis Duckworth, the men of the Black Arrow and the Duke of Gloucester and his soldiers celebrated with a dinner.

Richard and Joanna lived a happy, peaceful life in the forest, far from wars and battles.

1. **Abbey**：教堂。

UNDERSTANDING THE TEXT

1 SUMMARY

When did these things happen? Put the events on the correct part of the time arrow. The first one is done for you.

the past ←————————————————————————————

[B]　　　[ ]　　　[ ]　　　[ ]　　　[ ]　　　[ ]　　　[ ]

A Duckworth kills Sir Daniel.

B Duckworth sends Richard to meet the Duke of Gloucester.

C Richard and Joanna get married.

D Richard fights together with the Duke and saves his life.

E Richard finds Joanna.

F The Band of the Black Arrow join the Duke's men and fight at Shoreby Castle.

G The Duke knights Richard.

H York wins the battle at Shoreby.

KET

2 COMPREHENSION CHECK

What does the messenger say to Sir Oliver? Complete the conversation. Choose the right answers (A-H) to the questions (1-5). There are more answers than you need. There is an example at the beginning (0).

0	Who won the battle at Shoreby?	....F.....
1	What did Sir Daniel do?	....
2	What happened to the castle?	....
3	What happened to Shelton?	....
4	Is Bennet safe?	....
5	Where are Duckworth and Shelton now?	....

A It was destroyed.

B No. Duckworth killed him. He killed Sir Daniel, too.

C He escaped with Bennet and Joanna.

D He rescued Bennet.

E He fought bravely and the Duke knighted him.

F York.

G They're at Holywood.

H Lancaster.

A SECRET MESSAGE

Ellis Duckworth received this note from a mysterious messenger. Can you break the code to find out what it says?

> sift wyouf swanth otog ukilli boatesy, they hise shidings math ethey solde bchurche snears skettleys.

e.g.: s̶if̶t̶ = if

 FILL IN THE GAPS

Match the syllables in the box to make six words from Chapter Seven. Then use the words to complete what Ellis says to Richard.

mess	kni	sold	age	tle	ack
iers	tory	att	ght	vic	bat

Richard, take this important (**1**) .... to the Duke. If you see a (**2**) .... riding alone, that will be the Duke. Tell him that we will help him fight at the (**3**) .... tomorrow. Be careful! Sir Daniel's (**4**) .... are looking for us. They may (**5**) .... you. Good luck, Richard, and remember that (**6**) .... will soon be ours.

T: GRADE 4

 SPEAKING: HOLIDAYS

At the end of the story, Sir Daniel tries to escape to another country. Have you ever been to another country on holiday or to another city in your own country? Talk about it. Use these questions to help you.

- Where did you go?
- Why did you go there?
- Who did you go with?
- What did you enjoy about your trip?

6 PICTURE SUMMARY

Look at the pictures below and put them in the correct order. Then use the pictures to tell the story in your own words.

BEFORE YOU READ

1 VOCABULARY

Can you label the picture? Paragraphs 2, 3 and 4 of the dossier will help you.

1 ☐ helmet		2 ☐ shield		3 ☐ coat of arms	
4 ☐ sword		5 ☐ armour		6 ☐ squire	
7 ☐ page		8 ☐ horse			

Knights and the Knighthood Today

Today the title 'knight' refers to people who receive this honour from the king or queen. It is a 'thank you' for good services to the country. But in the Middle Ages a knight was a soldier who fought for the king and the country.

Knights in the Middle Ages almost always came from noble families. They had a high position [1] in society and worked for lords or directly for the king. When they went into battle they wore heavy armour and rode strong horses. They carried a special shield with their family's symbol, called a coat of arms.

When they weren't fighting in battles, knights often practised their skills by going to tournaments. [2] These were big competitions and there were several different sports including jousting. [3]

Knights jousting (1470-75) from Froissart's Chronicles.

1. **position**：地位。
2. **tournaments**：比賽；比武。
3. **jousting**：騎着馬用長矛比武。

Boys learnt how to become a knight from the age of seven. These young boys were called 'pages'. They learnt about horses and armour, and how to fight with a wooden sword. When they were around twelve they became 'squires'. A squire learnt how to fight from a real knight. He also helped the knight do many things, including putting on his armour before going into battle.

Today's knights do not need to fight and they do not have a specific job to do. The special honour is called a knighthood. In Great Britain, these awards are given twice a year. If you are knighted by the queen, you are then invited to a special ceremony [1] at Buckingham Palace. Here you kneel in front of the Queen and she touches your shoulders with a sword. A British man can then use 'Sir' before his name, and a British woman can use 'Dame' before hers. Sometimes the Queen awards an honorary knighthood to non-British citizens. These people are knighted but they cannot officially use the title. Recent examples are Bob Geldof and Bill Gates. Often non-famous people are given a knighthood to say 'thank you' for their charity [2] work.

1. **ceremony**：儀式。　　　　　　2. **charity**：慈善。

Dame Judi Dench.　　　　Sir Paul McCartney.

1 COMPREHENSION CHECK
Choose the best answer, A, B or C.

1 Who receives knighthoods today?
  A ☐ People who protect the Queen.
  B ☐ People who are born into rich families.
  C ☐ People who do something good for their country.

2 What is a coat of arms?
  A ☐ A protective suit made of metal.
  B ☐ A knight's family symbol.
  C ☐ A knight's jacket.

3 What was a tournament?
  A ☐ A battle.
  B ☐ A feast.
  C ☐ A competition.

4 Who was the youngest?
  A ☐ A squire.
  B ☐ A page.
  C ☐ A knight.

5 How often are knighthoods given today?
  A ☐ Once every six months.
  B ☐ Once a year.
  C ☐ Once every two years.

2 COMPREHENSION CHECK
Are these sentences true (T) or false (F)?

                                      T   F

1 Knights in the Middle Ages usually came from important, wealthy families. ☐ ☐
2 Squires taught pages how to fight. ☐ ☐
3 Today knighthoods are given by the Prime Minister. ☐ ☐
4 Every knight uses the title 'Sir'. ☐ ☐
5 Knights aren't always well-known people. ☐ ☐

3 READING PICTURES
Look at the pictures of modern-day knights on page 80. Answer these questions:

- What are they famous for?
- Why do you think they were knighted?
- Can you think of any non-famous people who deserve to become knights?

EXIT TEST 1

1 WORD GAME

Read the clues and write the name of each character in the spaces. Which character do the letters in the red boxes spell?

1   I kidnapped Joanna Sedley.
2   I'm the leader of the Band of the Black Arrow.
3   I'm really Joanna Sedley.
4   I'm a loyal friend of Ellis Duckworth.
5   I helped Joanna and Richard, but Duckworth killed me in the end.
6   I'm a religious man, but did I kill Richard's father? Perhaps!
7   My parents died when I was young. I was disguised as John Matcham.

2 COMPREHENSION CHECK

Read the sentences and find four things which didn't happen in the story.

A   Nick Appleyard is killed with a black arrow.
B   John Matcham escapes from Sir Daniel, but his horse gets hurt in the marsh.

C Richard and John see some of Sir Daniel's men sitting around a camp fire.
D Sir Daniel takes Richard and John back to his castle. He tells Richard to sleep in the room above the church.
E John tells Richard he is really Joanna Sedley. Richard escapes, but Joanna is still a prisoner.
F Richard tries to rescue Joanna from the house by the sea, but he fails.
G Richard and Ellis Duckworth put on friars' robes and visit Joanna at Shoreby Castle.
H At Joanna's wedding, a black arrow kills Lord Shoreby.
I Richard rescues the Duke of Lancaster and is knighted for his bravery.
J York wins the battle at Shoreby Castle.
K Sir Daniel escapes to France.

3 PLACES IN THE STORY
Where did these things happen? Choose A, B or C.

1 Sir Oliver finds a note on the church door.
  A ☐ Holywood
  B ☐ Kettley
  C ☐ Tunstall

2 John escapes from Sir Daniel.
  A ☐ Kettley
  B ☐ Holywood
  C ☐ Moat House Castle

3 Richard falls from the tower.
  A ☐ Moat House Castle
  B ☐ Shoreby Castle
  C ☐ The old church

4 Joanna meets Lord Shoreby.
  A ☐ Moat House Castle
  B ☐ Shoreby-on-the-Till
  C ☐ Kettley

5 York wins the final battle against Lancaster.
  A ☐ Kettley
  B ☐ Moat House Castle
  C ☐ Shoreby Castle

6 Joanna and Richard get married.
  A ☐ Moat House Castle
  B ☐ Kettley
  C ☐ Holywood

7 Sir Daniel is killed.
  A ☐ On the boat to France.
  B ☐ In the forest near Holywood.
  C ☐ In the battle at Shoreby Castle.

EXIT TEST 2

Answer the following questions about the story.

1 Why were the villagers so angry with Richard's news about the battle?
2 What did the letter on the church door say?
3 Describe Sir Daniel.
4 Where did Richard find John Matcham after he left the Sun Inn in Kettley?
5 What was Richard's father's name?
6 What was Sir Daniel wearing when Richard and John saw him in the forest?
7 What important question did Richard ask Sir Daniel about his father?
8 How did Richard and Joanna escape from the room above the church?
9 What adjectives did Ellis Duckworth use to describe Richard?
10 What were Sir Daniel and Lord Shoreby talking about near the sea?
11 How did Lawless and Richard enter Sir Daniel's castle in Shoreby without anyone recognising them?
12 How did they stop the marriage between Lord Shoreby and Joanna?
13 What happened when Richard took Ellis Duckworth's message to the Duke of Gloucester?
14 Did Ellis Duckworth use all four of the Black Arrows?

The Black Arrow

KEY TO
THE EXERCISES
AND EXIT TESTS

About the Author

Page 9 – exercise 1

1 F – he liked the stories which his father told him.
2 F – he started studying engineering but then he decided to study law.
3 F – his wife was American.
4 T
5 T
6 F – the warm weather helped him a lot.

Chapter ONE

Page 12 – exercise 1

1 village **2** message **3** priest

Page 12 – exercise 2

1 taxes **2** defend **3** loyal

Page 12 – exercise 3

1B **2**C **3**A

Page 18 – exercise 1

1C **2**A **3**A **4**C **5**B **6**B **7**A **8**C

Page 18 – exercise 2

1 handsome **2** angry **3** unfriendly
4 strange **5** brave **6** honest
7 dangerous **8** surprised

Page 19 – exercise 3

1C **2**G **3**E **4**D **5**B **6**A **7**F

Page 19 – exercise 4

1 ward **2** bell **3** battle **4** villagers
5 twenty **6** terrible **7** arrow
8 message **9** three **10** Hatch

Chapter TWO

Page 20 – exercise 1

1 marry **2** wife **3** get **4** marriage
5 husband **6** good **7** happy **8** money

Page 20 – exercise 2

1 & **2** open answers **3** He/she is asking for directions to go somewhere.

Page 26 – exercise 1

1B **2**A **3**C **4**B **5**B

Page 26 – exercise 2

John Matcham: sad, thin, young.
Sir Daniel Brackley: worried, bald, greedy, evil.
Richard Shelton: brave, hungry, thirsty, kind.

Page 27 – exercise 3

1E 2D 3A 4B 5F 6C

Page 27 – exercise 4

1 on 2 for 3 about 4 from 5 from
6 to 7 in 8 with

The Wars of the Roses

Page 28 – exercise 1

1C 2A 3B 4D

Page 28 – exercise 2

1 1455 2 1485 3 York 4 Lancaster
5 king of England 6 white rose 7 red rose

Page 32 – exercise 1

1A 2C 3D 4F 5B 6E

Chapter THREE

Page 33 – exercise 1

1E 2A 3D 4C 5B

Page 34 – exercise 2

Open answer.

Page 34 – exercise 3

1 Lawless and Ellis Duckworth.
2 They are eating and talking.
3 From a farmhouse near Kettley.
4 The Band of the Black Arrow has many friends.
5 He hears someone coming through the forest.
6 One of Sir Daniel's men.

Tapescript

Ellis: Lawless, isn't that food ready yet?
Lawless: Here you are Ellis, freshly cooked eggs for the first time in a month.
Ellis: Aaah. Well done Lawless. Where did you get the eggs from?
Lawless: From a farmhouse near Kettley. Don't worry Ellis, the Band of the Black Arrow has many friends. We will not be hungry.
Ellis: You're right Lawless. We have many loyal friends. There are many people that hate Sir Daniel Brackley and want to help the Band. They know Brackley is a cruel man.
Lawless: Just look what he did to your house Ellis.
Ellis: Yes. My dear home burnt down by Bennet Hatch. Well, he will pay for it.
Lawless: Listen Ellis. Someone's coming through the forest.
Ellis: I think it must be Daniel Brackley's men. Quick everyone, Hide and get ready to attack.

Page 34 – exercise 4

1 leader – Ellis Duckworth 2 enemy – Ellis Duckworth 3 attack – Ellis Duckworth 4 escape – Richard Shelton 5 truth – Richard Shelton

Page 41 – exercise 1

G F A E B D C

Page 41 – exercise 2

1C 2B 3A 4A 5B 6C 7B 8A

Page 42 – exercise 3

1G 2H 3A 4C 5D

Page 42 – exercise 4

1 the 2 a 3 – 4 a 5 the 6 a 7 the
8 an 9 the 10 a 11 an 12 an 13 a
14 a 15 a 16 the

Chapter FOUR
Page 43 – exercise 1

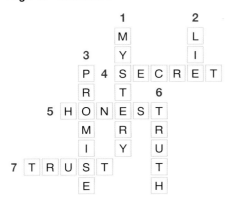

Page 43 – exercise 2

1 Richard is in his bedroom.
2 Richard is feeling confused and angry.
3 Open answer.

Chapter FOUR
Page 49 – exercise 1

Richard and John are now at Moat House Castle. Richard has a lot of questions. For example, he wants to know who killed his **(1) brother**. Bennet Hatch tells Richard to be careful. He also tells him not to trust **(2) John Matcham**.
Richard and Sir Daniel argue. Sir Daniel thinks Richard knows too much. That evening, some men take Richard to the room above the **(3) old theatre**. They tell him it's full of **(4) mice**!
John comes to Richard's room. He takes off his hat, and Richard understands that John is really a girl! Her name is Joanna Sedley. They find a secret trapdoor under **(5) the bed**. Bennet Hatch finds them. **(6) He doesn't help them escape**.

1 father   **2** Sir Daniel or Sir Oliver   **3** old church   **4** ghosts   **5** table   **6** He gives them the key to the door.

Page 49 – exercise 2
1E   **2**D   **3**A   **4**C   **5**B   **6**F

Page 50 – exercise 3
1A   **2**B   **3**B   **4**A   **5**C   **6**A   **7**C   **8**B

Tapescript

Joanna: My Parents died when I was only twelve.
Richard: How did they die?
Joanna: There was a terrible fire at my home, Cromby Hall
Richard: Oh, how awful. What happened?
Joanna: Only I escaped the fire. After that Lord Foxham, a good friend of my father, looked after me. Then one day, Sir Daniel invited us to a party at Moat House Castle. We went and Sir Daniel asked me to stay for a few weeks. I stayed but then he didn't let me leave.
Richard: How did you get away from him?
Joanna: Lord Foxham came with his soldiers. He ordered Sir Richard to let me go. Some years passed, Lord Foxham wanted me to marry Lord Hamley.
Richard: Hamley? But why?
Joanna: He was a good friend of Lord Foxham. Lord Foxham thought I would be happy with him. Hamley was a good man but very old. I didn't want to marry him.
Richard: Then what happened?
Joanna: Well, then Sir Daniel came one day with three of his soldiers. I was in the garden at Lord Foxham's house when they came and kidnapped me.

Page 51 – exercise 4
1 ghosts   **2** trapdoor   **3** corridor
4 kidnap   **5** tower

Chapter FIVE
Page 51 – exercise 1
1 rope   **2** stone   **3** prisoner

Page 51 – exercise 2
1B   **2**C   **3**A

Page 57 – exercise 1
1B   **2**A   **3**B   **4**C   **5**C   **6**A   **7**B   **8**B

Page 58 – exercise 2

Richard: brave, angry, loyal, dangerous
Joanna: beautiful, rich, young
Lord Shoreby: short, fat, old, greedy, bad
Sir Daniel Brackley: greedy, dishonest, bad

Page 58 – exercise 3

Dear Richard,
I am a prisoner in a house near the sea.
Brackley wants me to marry Shoreby.
Please rescue me. Be careful, my love.
Brackley is dangerous.
Joanna

Chapter Six
Page 59 – exercise 1

1 friar – A religious man. He usually lives with others in a monastery.
2 soldier – A man or woman in the army.
3 musician – A person that plays a musical instrument.
4 merchant – Someone who buys and sells things.
5 lord – A man who has a high position in society.
6 acrobat – An entertainer who does amazing tricks with his or her body.

Page 66 – exercise 1

1A 2A 3C 4C 5A 6A 7B 8C

Page 66 – exercise 2

1A 2C 3B 4G 5H 6F 7E 8D

Page 67 – exercise 3

Page 67 – exercise 4
Open answer.

Page 68 – exercise 5
1 went 2 could 3 met 4 was 5 told
6 put 7 saw 8 came

Chapter Seven
Page 68 – exercise 1
1E 2A 3D 4B 5C

Page 75 – exercise 1
B D F H G E A C

Page 75 – exercise 2
1C 2A 3E 4B 5G

Page 76 – exercise 3
If you want to kill Oates, he is hiding at the old church near Ketley.

Page 76 – exercise 4
1 message 2 knight 3 battle
4 soldiers 5 attack 6 victory

Page 76 – exercise 5
Open answer.

Page 77 – exercise 6
I H J B K D A L G C E F

Knights and the Knighthood Today
Page 78 – exercise 1
1B 2H 3G 4F 5A 6E 7D 8C

Page 81 – exercise 1
1C 2B 3C 4B 5A

Page 81 – exercise 2
1T 2T 3F 4F 5F

Page 81 – exercise 3
Open answer.

Page 82 – exercise 1

1 Daniel Brackley; **2** Ellis Duckworth; **3** John Matcham; **4** Lawless; **5** Bennet Hatch; **6** Oliver Oates; **7** Joanna Sedley; **Mystery character:** Richard Shelton.

Page 82 – exercise 2

C, G, I, K.

Page 83 – exercise 3

1 C; **2** A; **3** A; **4** B; **5** C; **6** C; **7** B.

Page 84

1 Because many men from the village died in the battles and their wives and children were hungry. They also paid high taxes to Sir Daniel.

2 It said that there were four black arrows. One killed Nick Appleyard, and the others were for Bennet Hatch, Sir Oliver Oates and Sir Daniel.

3 He was a tall man of about forty. He was bald with a big nose and black eyes. He was a very greedy man.

4 In the marsh.

5 Harry Shelton.

6 A friar's robe.

7 'Did you kill my father?'

8 They went through a trapdoor and down a long secret corridor.

9 Brave and loyal.

10 Lord Shoreby's marriage to Joanna.

11 They wore friar's robes.

12 Ellis Duckworth and his men killed Lord Shoreby with a black arrow.

13 Richard helped a young knight to fight the soldiers. He then discovered that this knight was the Duke of Gloucester.

14 No. He didn't kill Sir Oliver because he decided to live in peace.

 # NOTES

 # NOTES

 NOTES

NOTES

 NOTES

Black Cat English Readers

Level 1A
Peter Pan
Zorro!
American Folk Tales
The True Story of Pocahontas
Davy Crockett

Level 1B
Great Expectations
Rip Van Winkle and The Legend of Sleepy Hollow
The Happy Prince and The Selfish Giant
The American West
Halloween Horror

Level 1C
The Adventures of Tom Sawyer
The Adventures of Huckleberry Finn
The Wonderful Wizard of Oz
The Secret of the Stones
The Wind in the Willows

Level 1D
The Black Arrow NEW!
Around the World in Eighty Days NEW!
Little Women NEW!

Level 2A
Oliver Twist
King Authur and his Knights
Oscar Wilde's Short Stories
Robin Hood
British and American Festivities

Level 2B
David Copperfield
Animal Tales
The Fisherman and his Soul
The Call of the Wild
Ghastly Ghosts!

Level 3
Alice's Adventures in Wonderland
The Jumping Frog
Hamlet

The Secret Garden
Great English Monarchs and their Times

Level 4A
The £1,000,000 Bank Note
Jane Eyre
Sherlock Holmes Investigates
Gulliver's Travels
The Strange Case of Dr Jekyll and Mr Hyde

Level 4B
Romeo and Juliet
Treasure Island
The Phantom of the Opera
Classic Detective Stories
Alien at School

Level 5A
A Christmas Carol
The Tragedy of Dr Faustus
Washington Square
A Midsummer Night's Dream
American Horror

Level 5B
Much Ado about Nothing
The Canterbury Tales
Dracula
The Last of the Mohican
The Big Mistake and Other Stories

Level 6A
Pride and Prejudice
Robinson Crusoe
A Tale of Two Cities
Frankenstein
The X-File: Squeeze

Level 6B
Emma
The Scarlet Letter
Tess of the d'Urbervilles
The Murders in the Rue Morgue and the Purloined Letter
The Problem of Cell 13

BLACK CAT ENGLISH CLUB

Membership Application Form

BLACK CAT ENGLISH CLUB is for those who love English reading and seek for better English to share and learn with fun together.

Benefits offered:
- *Membership Card*
- *Member badge, poster, bookmark*
- *Book discount coupon*
- *Black Cat English Reward Scheme*
- *English learning e-forum*
- *Surprise gift and more...*

Simply fill out the application form below and fax it back to 2565 1113.

Join Now! It's FREE exclusively for readers who have purchased *Black Cat English Readers* !

The book(or book set) that you have purchased: _____

English Name: _____ (Surname) _____ (Given Name)

Chinese Name: _____

Address: _____

Tel: _____ Fax: _____

Email: _____
(Login password for e-forum will be sent to this email address.)

Sex: ❏ Male   ❏ Female

Education Background: ❏ Primary 1-3   ❏ Primary 4-6   ❏ Junior Secondary Education (F1-3)
❏ Senior Secondary Education (F4-5)   ❏ Matriculation
❏ College   ❏ University or above

Age: ❏ 6 - 9   ❏ 10 - 12   ❏ 13 - 15   ❏ 16 - 18   ❏ 19 - 24   ❏ 25 - 34
❏ 35 - 44   ❏ 45 - 54   ❏ 55 or above

Occupation: ❏ Student   ❏ Teacher   ❏ White Collar   ❏ Blue Collar
❏ Professional   ❏ Manager   ❏ Business Owner   ❏ Housewife
❏ Others (please specify: _____)

As a member, what would you like **BLACK CAT ENGLISH CLUB** to offer:

❏ Member gathering/ party   ❏ English class with native teacher   ❏ English competition
❏ Newsletter   ❏ Online sharing   ❏ Book fair
❏ Book discount   ❏ Others (please specify: _____)

Other suggestions to **BLACK CAT ENGLISH CLUB:**

_____

Please sign here: _____

(Date: _____)